THE ADVENTURES OF BOBBLES AND BETTY!

WHO IS BETTY?

BY PHILIP GARCIA

ILLUSTRATED BY SCRIBBLELINE

I'm Bobbles...

They call me naughty,
but I'm just having fun!

Join me in my adventures...

"BOBBLES!"

Mum and Dad stood in the doorway to the house, looking at the living room.

The sofa cushions were turned upside-down on the living room rug.

The pillows were on the dining room table.

The dining room chairs were scattered on the floor, their legs sticking up in the air.

The chandelier was still shaking back and forth.

A trail of dog food lay on the floor, leading from the living room to the kitchen.

Mum and Dad took a deep breath.
They knew Bobbles, their little white and black dog,
had caused yet another disaster!

"Oh, whatever will we do with him?" Mum asked.

Dad shrugged, shaking his head. "I don't know," he said sadly.

They walked in, putting down their shopping bags.

Mum followed the trail of food into the kitchen,
where she found a shredded box of cereal.

"Oh no," she said.

"Bobbles!" Mum said. "You get in here right now."

Bobbles came into the room, his head bent down to the floor.

"Someone was a naughty boy again," Dad said.
"Whatever, and I mean, whatever will we do with you?"

"Something has to change, Dad," Mum said.

"Yes, but what can we do?"

Mum and Dad started to clean up the mess,
while Bobbles, feeling guilty, whined and followed them.

"I know, boy," said Dad.
"You're a good doggy, but sometimes you get carried away."

"He needs a good influence," said Mum.
"Someone who... wait, I think I have an idea, Dad."

Bobbles and Dad turned to Mum.
She had a gleam in her eyes,
and soon they would find out what she meant.

A few days later, the sun shone brightly,
and birds chirped as Mum, Dad, and Bobbles got into the family car.

"Today's the day," Mum said.

Mum drove Dad and Bobbles to the dog kennel,
where they went inside. Bobbles was barking,
turning around in circles, looking at all the dogs.

"He's so excited!" said Mum.
"But don't worry, Bobbles, we're going to find a best friend for you."

Soon, they were meeting different dogs.
One was a big German Shepherd with brown eyes.

"Maybe he's too big," said Dad.

Another was a Greyhound,
with blues eyes and skinny, long legs.

"Maybe she's too fast," Mum said.

And on and on they went,
meeting new dogs.

Until finally,
Mum and Dad noticed Bobbles was missing.

"Bobbles?" said Dad.

"Where'd you go?"

But then they heard a familiar bark
that seemed to be saying,
"Over here! Over here!"

Mum and Dad ran over to find Bobbles
nuzzling the nose of a tiny beautiful dog
with curly black fur.
With fluffy floppy ears and big dark eyes,
she seemed to be a perfect choice.

"I think Bobbles found her," Dad said.
"He found his new best friend."

Mum smiled, and she, too, knew the truth.

And so, everyone went home together that night.

They've called me Betty Boo!

I wonder what adventures
we will have together?

Printed in Poland
by Amazon Fulfillment
Poland Sp. z o.o., Wrocław

53348100R00016